HOUNDED DOWN

(ILLUSTRATED)

BY G. H. TEED

(GEORGE HEBER HAMILTON TEED (1886-1938)

from *The Thriller* magazine, 30 May 1931, No. 121, Vol. 4

Stillwoods Edition

Stillwoods.Blogspot.Ca

Catalogue information:
Title: Hounded Down (Illustrated)
Illustrated by unknown.
Author: G. H. Teed (George Heber Hamilton Teed (1886-1938))
First published in: The Thriller magazine, 30 May 1931, No. 121, Vol. 4
This edition by: Stillwoods, 2018.
ISBN Canada: 978-1-988304-49-6
Blog: Stillwoods.Blogspot.Ca
Storefront: http://www.lulu.com/spotlight/lulubook22

Details: a crime and mystery novel with locale of 1930s, London, England.

Introduction:

George Heber Hamilton Teed, (1886-1938) at this point in research, is practically an unknown. We have been able to recover a few war records from Ancestry.Ca, but his birth information is still missing.

All the antidotal information informs us that he was born in New Brunswick, Canada and that he travelled extensively before, finally settling in England.

He is best known as a novelist, adding 'pulp' stories about 'Sexton Blake' a British sleuth, who is still revered on English websites next to Sherlock Holmes.

G. H. Teed's enlistment papers etc. follow. His last wife was called Ivy, and one interview with her, will be presented in a forthcoming publication. Note that GHT enlisted in London, thus no Canadian records seem to exist though he was apparently with a Canadian corps.

DESCRIPTIVE REPORT ON ENLISTMENT.

Applicable to all ranks.
(To correspond with Entries on the Medical History Sheet.)

Name _George Heber Hamilton Teed_

Apparent age _31_ years _____ months. Height _5_ feet _6 7/8_ inches.

Chest Measurement { Girth when fully expanded _38 1/2_ inches.
Range of expansion _3_ inches.

Distinctive marks _____

INFORMATION SUPPLIED BY RECRUIT.

Name and Address of next-of-kin _Mr. G.R. Teed. Woodstock_
N.B. Canada Relationship _Brother_

Particulars as to Marriage.

(a) Christian and Surname of Woman to whom married, and whether spinster or widow. (b) Place and date of marriage.
(c) Present address. (d) Signature of Officer verifying entry from Certificate.

(a)	(b)	(c)	(d)
			Verified from certificate.

Particulars as to Children.

Christian Names	Date and Place of Birth	(d)
		Verified from certificate.

MILITARY HISTORY SHEET.

1. Passed classes of Instruction †	
† This includes any authorised class of instruction, e.g., in swimming, chiropody, &c.	
2. Campaigns ... ... (including Actions)	
3. Wounded	
4. Special instances of gallant conduct and mentions in public despatches	

Name of Medal	Clasp
5. Medals, decorations and annuities ...	

6. Injuries in or by the service	

4

2096

MEDICAL HISTORY of— Hslov 9a/54?

Surname _Teed_   Christian Names _George Hebert Hamilton_

Direct
K.E.H.

TABLE I.—General Table.

Birthplace { Parish _Woodstock_
{ County _New Brunswick_

Examined { on day of **15 JAN 1918** 191
{ at **CENTRAL LONDON RECRUITING DEPOT, WHITEHALL, S.W.**

Declared Age _31_ years _days_

Trade or Occupation _Journalist_

Height _5_ feet _6 5/8_ inches.   Weight _157_ lbs.

Colour of _original dark_ Complexion _dark_

" Eyes _grey_

Chest Measurement { Girth when fully expanded } _38_ inches.
{ Range of expansion } _3_ inches.

Physical Development _good_

Vaccination Marks { Arm, RIGHT / LEFT
{ Number _0_ / _1_

When Vaccinated _Infancy_ 6

Vision { R.E.—V = _6/18_ } With { R. _4_
{ L.E.—V = _6/6_ } Glasses { L.

13/1/1918

Identification Marks, such as Tattoo, Moles, Scars, etc:—
Scar R leg, also L forehead

Defects or Ailments:—

Examined and found—

Fit for Grade { I.
{ II.
{ III.

(Strike out those which do not apply.)

Signature _J Bradshaw_   **15 JAN 1918**

NATIONAL SERVICE MEDICAL BOARD,
LONDON No. 3.

Re-examined for posting at

On day of 191
at _Central London Area_
Enlisted { _Scotland Yard_   14 JAN 1918
{ on day of 191

	Corps	Regtl. No.
Enlisted	1st King **Edward's Horse.**	_2096_
Transferred to		

W. P. Griffith & Sons Ltd., Printers, Old Bailey, E.C. 4.
[1524] W0 74/PP127 250m 10/17a 45 G & S 59

TABLE III.—Boards, Courts of Enquiry, Vaccination, Inoculations, etc.; Examination for Field or Foreign Service; Extension of engagement, or Prolongation of Service; Issue of Surgical Appliances, Particulars of Dental Treatment, etc.

Date	Brief details
	Heart
	Normal
	Lungs

	DATE OF EXAM. 1, 2, 3	DATE OF ISSUE	FRAME No.	WIDTH MEASUREMENTS		VISION WITHOUT GLS	AXIS	CYL	SPH	REMARKS	SIGNATURE OF M.O.
RANK & NAME R L											
CORPS R L											
VISION WITH GLS R L											

2-II-18   V.R.E. 6/18 L.E. 6/6

There is mixed astigmatism
is in right eye.   Glasses
will be supplied. I.C.
Examined before a medical Board
Report unfit for further Service

Remarks: Vision fit for Grade I

TABLE IV.—Service Table.

Station or Troopship	Date of arrival or embarkation	Date of departure or disembarkation

Became non-effective by _Discharge_
on _10th_ day of _April_
(Signature) _Crowther_
(Rank) _S/o Cav. Records_

KING GEORGE Vth HOSPITAL
20 MAR 1918
DUBLIN

5

Direct Enlistment From Canada NB

Forms
B. 2505

Army Form B. 2505.

Isla NA 547

SHORT SERVICE. A

(For the Duration of the War.)

ATTESTATION OF

No. **2096** Name **TEED G.H.H.** Corps **1st King Edward's Horse,**

Questions to be put to the Recruit before Enlistment.

1. What is your Name?	*George Heber Hamilton Teed*
2. In or near what Parish or Town were you born?	2. In the Parish of *Woodstock,* in or near the Town of *New Brunswick* in the County of
3. What is your full Address? LONDON WHITEHALL JAN 1918 No. 3945	3. *Woodstock. N.B Canada*
4. Are you a British Subject?	4. *Yes*
5. What is your Age?	5. *31* Years Months
6. What is your Trade or Calling?	6. *Journalist*
7. Are you Married?	7. *No*
8. Have you ever served in any branch of His Majesty's Forces, naval or military? If so,* state particulars (i.e., if you have served in any of the Military Forces your regimental number, regiment, date, and cause of discharge)	*Canadian Militia 4 Yrs.*
9. Have you truly stated the whole, if any, of your previous service?	9. *Yes*
10. Are you willing to be vaccinated or re-vaccinated?	10. *Yes*
11. Are you willing to be enlisted for General Service?	11. *Yes*
12. Did you receive a Notice, and do you understand its meaning, and who gave it you?	12. *Yes* (Name) *S.S.M Fegan* Corps *1st K.E.H*
13. Are you willing to serve upon the following conditions, provided His Majesty should so long require your services? For the duration of the War, at the end of which you will be discharged with all convenient speed. If employed with Hospitals, depots of Mounted Units, and as Clerks, &c., you may be retained after the termination of hostilities until your services can be spared, but such retention shall in no case exceed six months?	13. *Yes*

George Heber Hamilton Teed do solemnly declare that the above answers made by me to the above questions are true, and that I am willing to fulfil the engagements made.

George Heber Hamilton Teed, SIGNATURE OF RECRUIT.

A Hamilton Signature of Witness.

OATH TO BE TAKEN BY RECRUIT ON ATTESTATION.

George Heber Hamilton Teed swear by Almighty God that I will be faithful and bear true Allegiance to His Majesty King George the Fifth, His Heirs, and Successors, and that I will, as in duty bound, honestly and faithfully defend His Majesty, His Heirs, and Successors, in Person, Crown, and Dignity against all enemies, and will observe and obey all orders of His Majesty, His Heirs, and Successors, and of the Generals and Officers set over me. So help me God.

CERTIFICATE OF MAGISTRATE OR ATTESTING OFFICER.

The Recruit above named was cautioned by me that if he made any false answer to any of the above questions he would be liable to be punished as provided in the Army Act.

The above questions were then read to the Recruit in my presence.

I have taken care that he understands each question, and that his answer to each question has been duly entered as replied to, and the said Recruit has made and signed the declaration and taken the oath before me at *Central London Area*

on this_____ day of **24 JAN 1918** 19   *Nr Scotland Yard*

Signature of the Justice

† Certificate of Approving Officer.

I certify that this Attestation of the above-named Recruit is correct, and properly filled up, and that the required forms appear to have been complied with. I accordingly approve, and appoint him to the ‡ *1st King Edwards Horse*

If enlisted by special authority, Army Form B. 203 (or other authority for the enlistment) will be attached to the original attestation.

Date **28 January** 19 **18**.

Place **Dublin**

W. B. Wadham Captain

Adjutant, Reserve Regiment,
1st King Edward's Horse

} Approving Officer.

† The signature of the Approving Officer is to be affixed in the presence of the Recruit.
‡ Here insert the "Corps" for which the Recruit has been enlisted.

* If so, the Recruit is to be asked the particulars of his former service, and to produce, if possible, his Certificate of Discharge and Certificate of Character, which should be returned to him conspicuously endorsed in red ink, as follows, viz.—(Name)_____
re-enlisted in the (Regiment)_____ on the (Date)_____

HOUNDED

With a sudden sweep, the garage doors swung open and Dimmock trod on the accelerator. A roar, and the car hurled forward into the midst of the waiting gangsters.

DOWN

by G.H. Teed

SENSATIONAL NEW
MYSTERY NOVEL

DIMMOCK saw, obliquely, that the tiny, green-frosted bulb in the fender glowed twice. Without lowering his book he watched for the third flash. It did not come.

His hand went stealthily across to the revolving bookcase that stood close to the easy-chair in which he lounged. His fingers closed on the butt of the loaded, automatic pistol that hung from the wooden peg he had fixed inside some months before.

Yet not for a moment did he take his gaze from the bulb in the fender. It remained dead, almost indistinguishable in the scroll work of the steel.

He slid out of the soft embrace of the deep chair and got to his feet. He stood listening, still watching the bulb. When he was satisfied that it would reveal nothing further, he glanced towards the door.

Then his gaze swept slowly round the cosily furnished living-room of the cottage where he had buried himself eighteen months before. Everything seemed perfectly normal. But he knew the green bulb had not been flashed by accident. Creed would not blunder like that.

He crossed the room quietly and stepped into the small hall. It was lit by a single stand-lamp that stood on a table near the front door. Nothing here.

He entered the dining-room, which was in darkness. He stood again, listening. The faint clatter of a train emerging from the cutting two miles away was all that broke the stillness.

The hands of the alarm clock on the mantelpiece stood at five minutes past midnight. Creed must have pressed the signal as nearly as possible on the hour.

Against one wall was a small battery of switches. Dimmock dragged down the lever that controlled them. The immediate effect was to extinguish the bulb in the kitchen, but to reveal a white glare against the drawn blind.

Dimmock strode across the room, his movements swifter and more definite now. He jerked the blind up and looked out into a Sussex garden that was illuminated almost as brightly as if the sun were shining. A dozen powerful bulbs hung from trees that showed leaves still glistening from the drizzle that had been falling all day.

Dimmock recrossed the room and stepped into the short passage that led to the back door. Whatever was to be disclosed should be outside.

He was right. The answer was there in the form of a man sprawled out on the wet semicircle of bricks that projected from the threshold. His head, barren of hair as an egg, lay over the edge of the brick, temple and one ear in the mud; the tip of his wooden leg almost touched the sill of the door.

Dimmock was a distinct target for attack as he stood staring down at his manservant. He was not particularly tall, something over middle height, but he was broad, stockily, powerfully built. His bulk made an appreciable blur in the doorway.

Here, at the back, the flood lighting stretched over the hedge at the foot of the garden, and washed up against the trees at the far side of the six-acre field. Half a dozen men, a dozen, a score, could find plenty of cover behind the hedge.

But Dimmock did not attempt to shield himself. Someone had already got Creed; it looked as if he had been "bumped off." It disposed of his only human outpost, so to say.

He bent over the prone man and got his arms underneath. He half carried, half dragged him across the bricks into the passage. There, he let him rest until he closed the door. It would have been on the cards for someone to start pumping bullets from behind the hedge. The menacing silence worried him.

He got Creed into the kitchen and pushed the switch lever up. The flood lighting outside vanished; the bulb that hung from the ceiling came on.

Dimmock pulled down the blind and gave his attention to the man on the floor. He was lying on his back, a long, livid scar dividing his barren scalp in half. He had got that when he had lost a leg in the Boxer Rebellion in China.

His eyes were closed, his thin-lipped mouth open a little. His face was ashen, but, then, it had never been any other hue since Dimmock had known him. His long body looked thinner, more bony than ever; his big hands were still out-thrust from the body, as if he had been reaching for something when he dropped.

Dimmock tested heart and pulse. The man was still alive. He turned him over and found a reddish bruise on the back of the skull. The blow had found blood-vessels beneath even that tight-drawn skin.

He busied himself with restoratives. Creed's eyes were open and his limbs were twitching when the telephone in the sitting-room rang suddenly.

With a quick assurance to the still muddled man on the floor, Dimmock hastened to answer it.

He had a hunch, before he lifted the receiver, what voice he should hear coming over the wire. He was not mistaken. It was the voice of a woman whose drawl was faintly tinged with an American accent.

"I've been trying all the evening to get a chance to 'phone you," he heard the voice saying, without any preliminary. "I've only got a few moments. They're going to isolate you and make you talk. If you don't—"

The voice went off abruptly. He called twice, urgency in his tones. He waggled the hook up and down. There was no telltale click. The line was as dead as mutton.

He slid the receiver on to the hook and got up. In the same moment the light in the sitting-room went out. Now he knew what the voice had meant. Isolate him— cut the telephone line, cut the lights. It had been done.

Make him talk, the voice had said. Would they? It could mean only one thing —Nita Ligan—the Shanghai Poppy. He had fallen for her, and she had double-crossed him before you could say knife.

Well, he'd got his own back all right. But she had spoiled his racket in Shanghai —the sweetest little racket a man ever played. And that bunch of highbinders of hers had hounded him out of the place, hounded him out of Hong Kong, hounded him out of Saigon, hounded him off the China coast.

He knew, three weeks ago, that they had come to England; that same voice he had heard to-night had warned him. Who was she? What was she doing, trailing around with that bunch? There had been something vaguely familiar about the accent, something like that of the girl he had pulled out of that nasty rumpus in the Willow Pattern Tea-house in the Bubbling Well Road. But why was she double-crossing the Shanghai Poppy in warning him? Was it another plant?

They weren't going to catch him like a rat in a wire trap. Make him talk, and then bump him off—maybe. He still had a shot or two in the locker.

He drew the automatic from the side pocket of his coat and stole stole the hall. He could hear Creed in the kitchen, his voice hoarse and querulous. He hissed a warning, and felt along the wall of the hall until he found the door of the tiny cloak-room.

He got hat and coat and donned them. In the kitchen again he bent over Creed.

"Can you walk?"

"I can manage. What is it? They jumped me before I could do a thing."

"How did they come?"

"Off the roof of the kitchen, came down the slope; must have been up there a long time. What's wrong with the lights?"

"Cut—so is the telephone. We've got to get out of here. Come on, up with you. Don't make a racket with that stump of yours. They will be on top of the place any moment now."

He drew Creed's arm across his shoulders and got him, awkwardly, into the passage. His right arm was swinging free. He had thrust the gun back into his pocket.

On the left, at the end of the passage opposite the back door, was another door which Dimmock had had cut when he first came to the place. It opened into a covered way that led along to the garage. This connecting link was, he always figured, the weakest in his chain of defence.

There were no windows, and the walls were of brick. Nevertheless, while he was in it, he was cut off from both house and garage.

He made the distance as swiftly as he could carry Creed along with him. He needed no light. He knew every inch of the way. He had rehearsed this get-away time and again until he was part perfect.

At the other end he groped in the blackness until he found the button that released the door there. He urged Creed into the garage and slid the door until he heard the spring-lock click. The faint sound was final. There was no going back now.

Still, supporting Creed he moved ahead cautiously until his outstretched hand came into contact with what he knew was the back of the car. He laid his lips close to Creed's ear.

"Get in and sit tight. If they're outside we'll go through them. Get your gun ready and use it if they swarm. Not so much noise with that stump of yours."

He got Creed into the back of the car, and, feeling his way along, climbed into the front. He felt about with his foot until it rested on the self-starter; he slid his hands along the curve of the wheel as if to reassure himself. Then he removed his right hand, took out his gun once more, laid it between his hip and the side, and, feeling through the darkness, caught hold of a lever that was fixed to the wall a foot or so away.

Then he sat tense, waiting.

The crash must come soon. If they were out there why didn't they get on with the job? It didn't matter how many; they wouldn't come unless they had him properly taped. There'd be enough of them to watch every point.

The Shanghai Poppy must have brought the whole gang with her—Costa and Silva, the two half-castes; those three Chinese that were always hanging about when she used to go to the Capitol in the Szechwan Road. That was before she had roped in old Ligan, but, even after that farce of a marriage, they had always been in evidence.

They didn't count. It was Kiley—Sam Kiley. He was the snake that would strike out of the darkness. She and Kiley and their knock-out drops and the killing they had planted on him.

He began to breathe more quickly at the thought. He had been willing to fade away, to keep what he had seized and let them stew. But if they wouldn't have it, if that she-devil thought she was going to lift off him what he'd brought away from the bungalow that night, when old Ligan had been bumped off, she had another think coming to her. It was just as well it had come to a show-down even if it was in England, where the gun stuff wasn't popular. He'd turn hunter and he'd fix Kiley.

His thoughts broke off as, from outside, a slight sound reached him. It was for all the world as if someone had stepped on a twig. He could hear the rustle of Creed's movements as he shifted his position. He took his hand from the lever and pushed it back, warningly. Then his fingers caught the smooth metal again, and he prepared to make the break.

A long minute passed during which not a sound broke the stillness. Then, again, something stirred outside. Followed a sudden racket, muffled by distance. They were at the house. They would be inside in no time now.

He pressed his foot on the self-starter. It ground, the engine throbbed; Dimmock dragged back on the lever. The single door of the garage, balanced to perfect response and powerfully sprung, opened with a sudden sweep.

The car was already moving. Someone crashed into the door and cursed. Then a shout broke almost in Dimmock's ear as the car slid over the threshold.

It gathered speed, headed towards the wide gates that, like the garage door, had swung open to the action of the lever. The man at the wheel crouched low. Two figures sprang after the car, and bullets began to sing overhead, to thud into the body of the vehicle.

Not much noise; they were using silencers. Creed held his reply. Dimmock got into second, brought the car on to the side-road outside, straightened out, got into third, then swung into the main road and, passing a stationary car, sped London-wards like a bat out of the pit.

As Dimmock dashed out into the open, he saw Creed sprawled out motionless on the doorstep.

AT the end of a mews, behind one of the short, narrow streets that be in the immediate angle formed by Baker Street and the Marylebone Road, stands a converted coach-house.

It formed, originally, part of a large and well-built estate, for its Georgian front is distinctly superior in workmanship to the other buildings which line each side of the mews.

The ground floor is a garage; the upper has been turned into a flat with modern improvements. Nor are the conveniences all to be reckoned inside if it means anything to a tenant to have more than one means of approach and departure.

At the back one can step into an old, disused graveyard. The gate in the iron railings that separate this almost forgotten retreat from the street is padlocked; but the rusty iron lock is so primitive of design that it is a simple matter to open it.

The accommodation in the flat is by no means extensive. There is a small sitting-room, a dining-room of equally restricted area, a tiny kitchen and three small bedrooms; enough, however, for one whose household is not large. And privacy may be a great asset.

At that hour in the morning when London seems to pause before starting the turn of another day, a woman sat in one of two easy-chairs that were drawn up before the fire in the sitting-room. She was young and decidedly attractive in a vividly exotic way.

Her hair was amazingly red, her pale face "made-up" with no little artistry, even the nostrils being tinted. A green velvet dress clung alluringly to her beautifully made body. Her necklace and rings were good, a little too "heavy," if one might be ultra-critical.

She was smoking, had been devouring cigarette after cigarette for the better part of two hours. Her gaze was almost constantly fixed on the closed door; her head was turned slightly towards the window.

The little silver clock on the mantelpiece had just chimed the quarter-past four when she sat up suddenly, her stare intensified. She saw the handle of the door turn, watched while it swung open almost noiselessly. She relaxed at sight of the man whose method of entry was so silent.

He was small, compact, lithe. His coal-black hair was varnished and plastered flat to his head. His face was white like that of one who sees little of the sun. His brown eyes and his wide smile were united in smooth suavity; his voice was soft and slick as an oiled bearing.

"You waited up," was what he said, when he had closed the door.

"Of course; well?"

Her voice slurred a little, had a hint of American accent mixed in it. His was stronger with the same origin.

"It was a fade-out."

Her lips curled in a faint sneer.

"What's the matter with you, Sam? You had him all taped, hadn't you?"

"Sure we had. But he was all set to get started, and, believe me, when he did start he kept moving."

"Why didn't you stop him? You had plenty of guns with you. What do you want him to do—walk up to you and say: 'Were you looking for me, Mr. Kiley? Please bump me off if you have the fancy.' Is that it?"

The smile did not leave his face; but his eyes held hers in silence. A full minute passed. The woman shifted uneasily, her gaze remaining fixed on his as if held by some fascination she could not break. At last she gasped and struggled to sit up.

"Don't, Sam, don't," she burst out, "don't look at me like that."

"I don't think we will have any more wise-cracking, baby," he said softly. "Papa might get cross, and that isn't— healthy."

She relaxed.

"I'm sorry, Sam. But I counted so on this. I thought you'd get him to-night."

"And so I would if he hadn't been primed to make the quickest get-away I've ever seen."

"What happened?"

"We closed in soon after dark. Chan got on to the roof from the front porch. Then we had a long wait; there was traffic passing on the main road. I wasn't taking any chances. It was along about midnight before I gave Chan the signal. He came down the roof and laid Creed out like a charm. Creed must have made some signal to Dimmock. I don't know; I'm puzzled about that."

"Why?"

"Because the place was suddenly lit up and Dimmock popped out almost at once. He hauled Creed into the house. I could have picked him off easily enough, but that would be a fool play before we made him talk. Lee Yeng cut the wires; Costa and Silva were each under a window, and Costa says he heard Dimmock talking to someone. It must have been to Creed, but if that is so he must have come round pretty soon. I'm puzzled about that, too!"

"What delayed you then?"

"Nothing. We closed in, and had just got one of the windows open when Dimmock burst out of the garage in his car. The door was a trick affair. It knocked Silva and Lee Yeng over, and, before they could get shooting properly, Dimmock was away. We couldn't get going quick enough to follow him."

"Did you find anything?"

"Not a thing. I went through that place with a fine tooth-comb. Where the stuff is salted isn't there; I'm sure of that now. Have you heard anything from Charlie?"

"He's still in the East End."

"Well, I'm certain Dimmock has a hideout somewhere down there."

"If he has, Charlie will find it."

"And when I trail Dimmock again I'll get him so hard he'll only have time to spill what we want to know before he pikes out. Just the same, there's something queer about this business. I've been thinking."

"What do you mean?"

"How could that bird be so quick on the uptake? Answer me that. How comes it he gets away from scratch so smooth, huh?"

"He knew we'd follow him."

"Of course he did. But that guy isn't going to sit on the doorstep night and day for eighteen months. I tell you, he knows we have been in this country for some weeks. He knew before to-night that we had located him. He was expecting us; he was all ready for the big break. How did he know, huh? Tell me that."

She frowned at him in sharp concentration.

"What do you mean?"

The gunman turned his head and glanced towards the door. Then he leaned forward so his whisper would reach her.

"Where is the kid?"

"In bed."

"How is she going it to-night?"

"She's been sniffing hard. She left me at the restaurant to go to the cloak-room; said she couldn't stand it any longer."

"If that kid sniffs as much coke as she seems to get away with, I don't know how she stands up under it," he said slowly. "What time did she pull off that stunt at the restaurant?"

"I can't say exactly—getting on for mid-night."

"How long was she gone?"

"Ten minutes or quarter of an hour."

"Huh! It don't take her that long to snuff a whiff of coke."

"What do you mean, Sam?"

"She had time, if she'd wanted, to get a trunk call through to Dimmock, didn't she? The line would be clear at that hour. That's what I mean. You might find out something from the cloak-room attendant. I tell you someone is double-crossing us; someone is keeping Dimmock piped. Who is it?"

The woman came to her feet.

"Wait for me," she said swiftly.

Kiley lit a fresh cigarette and listened. He could hear Nita's quick, light tap on a door; then her voice. He nodded at the fire.

"We'll find out what that kid is up to," he was telling himself, when he heard a quick rush of feet along the hall. The door burst open and he swung round to see Nita Ligan standing on the threshold, her red-lined nostrils working from some strong emotion.

"She's not there, Sam; she's gone."

Sam Kiley always maintained that he had been born in San Francisco. There was no certainty on that point. All he was positive about was finding himself as an urchin on the Barbary Coast when the dives along that lurid and notorious thoroughfare were running with the lid off.

He had learned a good many things there, not least of which had been to move fast when danger threatened. This accomplishment had carried him safely through the various criminal strata of most of the cities in America, in London, in Paris and, more recently, on the China coast.

At the astonishing news which Nita Ligan communicated he proved himself capable of exhibiting it still. He did not question her. He knew she had plenty of reason for her statement.

He was out of the room in a flash. A door at the end of the narrow hall communicated with a staircase that led down to the garage. At the top was a switch which he pulled down as he passed.

He plunged into the garage and made for the car. Just before reaching it he drew up and gave vent to a soft curse. His eyes were fixed on the near front wheel. He circled the car rapidly, scrutinising each tyre. All four were flat. On each wheel the valve rubber had been torn clean away.

Kiley started to return to the flat. He saw Nita Ligan on the bottom step. One finger was on her lips; she was pointing towards the door that led to the disused graveyard. His gaze jerked in the same direction. His hand dropped to his pocket as he saw the door open, slowly, a stealthy force behind it.

Then he relaxed, as an undersized Chinese in European clothes slipped in and closed the door after him. He smiled affably at sight of the two who waited. Kiley beckoned him forward urgently.

"What brings you here now, Charlie?"

The Chinese turned a mild eye upon him.

"I come like Miss 'Ilda say," he answered in tolerable English, but with the accent one hears in Honolulu—a place which Charlie Sin had had to leave for the good of his health.

"Missee Hilda—what time did she tell you that?"

"Maybe one o'clock."

"Where did you see her?"

"I telephone."

"Sweet jessamine!"

Kiley whirled round.

"One o'clock—what about that, Nita? You were here. What about this telephoning of Charlie's?"

Her brows were knit; her teeth were gnawing at her lower lip.

"The telephone rang. I was in my room. It was just after we got back from the restaurant. I asked her what it was; she said someone had the wrong number." Kiley turned back to the Chinese.

"What did you tell her? Get it out quick. What did you tell her?"

"I tell her wheah Dimmock have his hide-out."

Kiley seized him by the shoulder. His pale face was now a dead white.

"Tell me, tell me, tell me—where is it?"

Charlie Sin was frightened. Charlie Sin told him. Kiley released him and pushed past Nita, taking the steps two at a time. He was back in a moment or two, struggling into his coat, fuming as he came.

"At one o'clock she gets the office from Charlie where the hide-out is located. She tells you she is going to bed. She's going to take a whiff of coke and fade away. I knew we were being double-crossed. She's fooled you to a fare-thee-well, Nita. Coke! If that stuff she has been sniffing is any stronger than bicarbonate of soda, I'll eat all you can find. Keep Charlie here—and the others when they turn up."

"Where are you going, Sam?"

"I'm going to find that little snitch before she connects with Dimmock."

Kiley glared down at the girl malevolently. Nita shuddered. "Don't, Sam, don't," she cried. "Don't look at me like that."

AT a certain point on the river that gives it a commanding view of Limehouse Reach, there stands, almost unchanged from the roystering days of the second Charles, an inn with the somewhat expressive name: "Sailor, Come Home."

It is a place of dim interior, uneven floors, low beams, and many bewildering corridors that meander in seemingly aimless manner from one level to another—little, short flights of dark stairs linking them together as if they had met haphazard.

The inn is a place of considerably greater accommodation than one would surmise from the outside, though it has a good frontage to the street and a triple-galleried back on the river where, on a summer's afternoon, it is very pleasant to sit and smoke and lazily watch the big ships coming up to London Pool, or churning down on their way to the Seven Seas.

The ground floor public-rooms of the place consist of a dance-room, with small tables scattered round the edge of the floor and in many cunningly contrived alcoves; a large, well-stocked saloon bar for the better run of customers; a less ornate public bar for lascars, Malays and negroes, and a couple of private parlours for captains and mates.

For the bulk of the clients of this quite unique inn are seafaring men, or those connected in some way with that calling.

And, literally hiding walls and ceilings of these ground-floor rooms is a most amazing collection of curios and relics. Every country in the world has contributed some strange object to enhance the display which Mother Hooly has been amassing during her twenty-five years or so as proprietress of the Sailor, Come Home.

Reproductions of great paintings, Chinese curios in abundance, vases, caskets, inlaid and lacquered, shrunken human skulls from South America, old prints, stuffed birds of exotic hue, stuffed alligators and crocodiles, spears, whole turtle shells of extraordinary beauty, head-dresses, masks, and even totem poles. There is nothing like it anywhere else in London; it is probably unique in the world.

Nor could one find a more amazing "hostess" than Mother Hooly. She was a gigantic Portuguese-Chinese half-caste, who, before coming to London for some inscrutable reason more than a quarter of a century before, had been known by a far more expressive name in

23

the Portuguese colony of Macao at the mouth of the Canton River. Why she had embarked on the turgid stream of East London was her own secret.

In that time her place had become the recognised meeting-place for men in from the Seven Seas. All the ends of the world met at Mother Hooly's. It was to be ranked as much the cross-roads as Singapore or Hong Kong or Panama or 'Frisco; and Mother Hooly was the signpost with whom few would care to try conclusions. Six feet three in height, of astounding breadth and girth, she had the strength of three roughnecks, a cold courage that set her heavy features repellantly, an amazing quickness of foot and hand, and yet, locked away beneath that enormous bosom, a streak of sentiment as squashy as that of any unsophisticated schoolgirl.

It was rarely that any guests occupied the low-ceilinged rooms on the upper floors. Now and then a favoured sea captain would be found ensconced in one of them during his brief stay ashore. And, again, Mother Hooly would take others to her own private quarters for long conversations, which were carried on in whispers and in the gloom.

There were rumours, of course, but nothing definite. One might gather, in some mysterious way, that Mother Hooly's was a clearing-house for drugs, opium particularly.

One might catch a vagrant whisper that a good deal of illicit spirits found their way through that building from the river. And, if one kept one's ear close to the sounding board, one might catch a murmur which said that many a secret of the sea had its genesis in that same inn, was executed on the high seas, and saw its ending back within those walls.

Perhaps the mysterious conferences in her private quarters might have thrown some light on these whispers; or, on the other hand, they might have embraced nothing more than a friendly chat between Mother Hooly and some favoured customer.

Whichever it was, the persons who visited the giantess in those dim quarters never talked of what passed, though a keen observer would have discovered that for some time after they were always well provided with money.

Between five and six o'clock on a summer morning, when the London streets near the river were hazily obscured by a mist that hung from the cross on St. Paul's to earth, three persons sat in Mother Hooly's inner sanctum.

It was an unusual hour for the giantess to go into conference, her favourite hours for receiving her mysterious visitors being during the afternoon or between midnight and two o'clock.

But unusual events had persuaded her to alter her usual schedule, and, for half an hour or more—ever since the arrival of Peter Dimmock and Bill Creed—she had been sunk in a huge chair like some incredible monstrosity from another planet, giving heed to what the scarred man with the wooden leg was saying.

It was, curiously enough, he who seemed to carry the situation along. It was he who spoke for Dimmock; it was he whose urgent demands appeared to rouse no resentment in the giantess, usually so ready to sweep away, with one enormous hand, all suggestions made to her.

Dimmock was learning a little, but he still did not understand how it was that Creed could demand and receive of this human freak called Mother Hooly.

He knew that Creed had known her years and years ago in Macao. He told himself it must be on account of something that had taken place there. But that did not explain why mention of old Tom Ligan acted like a spur to send her heavy eyes swimming with smouldering fire.

It was sufficient for him that he could use the place as a hide-out for the time being. Creed had taken him to it months before, when they had first come to England.

Since then he had kept a room rented in case of just such an emergency as this, though when or how the rent was paid he didn't know. Creed attended to that; Creed, who, for some inscrutable reason, had attached himself to Dimmock back in Shanghai, when it was said openly that he had murdered old Tom Ligan.

Creed was still talking when, suddenly, the giantess held up one hand. All three sat in dead silence. Even the white cat on the wide window sill seemed to freeze to a statue.

Sounds that Mother Hooly had heard readied Dimmock's ears. They seemed to come from the wall—faint, quick, staccato rappings, as if someone were tapping on the other side of the panelling.

They grew more and more distinct; they came to a sudden end. Mother Hooly had come to her feet with the smooth agility that was so remarkable in one of her vast bulk. She was facing a curtain that hung against one wall between the fireplace and the corner.

It was about the only area in the room that was not concealed by an overflow of curios from the public-rooms, or rows upon rows of framed photographs of the army of sea captains who had passed through the place on their march through life during the past quarter of a century.

She still held one hand aloft. Creed signed to Dimmock, and the two rose. They had just stood upright when, with one great sweeping motion, Mother Hooly flung the curtain aside.

Smooth panelling was revealed. She laid her fingers against it and slid it aside almost noiselessly. The growing dawn showed Dimmock a short passage, with a closed door on the right and another at the end.

Now he could hear a tapping against the latter. Mother Hooly started towards it, but before she covered two strides there came a second staccato rattle, louder, more rapid than the sounds Dimmock had heard before. He knew it for the rattle of a gun.

The giantess covered the short distance to the door with a spring that would have done credit to a tigress. Dimmock was close at her heels. Creed was coming along in the rear, trying to swing on the tip of his wooden leg without noise.

Mother Hooly flung open the door. Under her arm, Dimmock saw the huddled form of a girl on the cobbles of the narrow side passage which the door served and which ran between the end of the inn and a blank warehouse wall from street to river-bank, being shut off from the short jetty back of the inn by a stout gate, kept padlocked.

Dimmock uttered a sharp exclamation and slid past the half-caste, bending over the girl. An oath broke from him as he recognised her as the girl he had known in the Willow Pattern Tea-house in Shanghai. Somebody had put her on the spot.

Mother Hooly pushed him aside and got her arms under the unconscious girl. Dimmock clawed out his gun and turned to run up the alley. The assassin couldn't have got far yet. But before he had taken a stride the ham-like hand of the giantess caught him by the shoulder and flung him back into the passage with as little effort as if he had been a sack of feathers.

"Fool," she snarled, "do you want the police in on this?"

She was holding the girl in the crook of one arm, and now she backed in through the door, taking care that her bulk prevented

Dimmock or Creed from getting out.

She closed the door and swept them along into the inner room. Creed closed the panel and dropped the curtain. Still carrying her burden, Mother Hooly led the way along a maze of narrow corridors and connecting staircases which had Dimmock guessing.

At last she pushed open the door of a room, and, by the light that came in through the window, Dimmock saw it was a small bed-room.

The giantess laid the girl on the bed and straightened up. Her eyes swept Dimmock and Creed, but she didn't see them. Suddenly she turned and made for the door, pausing only long enough to warn them to remain where they were.

She was no more than gone when, from somewhere below, came a slow, ponderous, authoritative knocking. Dimmock and Creed stood suddenly breathless and motionless.

With a swift movement, he whipped out his gun and jammed it against the crook's side. "Got you, Kiley," he snapped. "Keep your gang off."

JUST before mid-day Mother Hooly sent Creed to fetch Dimmock from his room to take him to Hilda Grey.

He had thrown himself on his own bed to think, but the more he tried to get a proper focus on the events of the past few hours, the more his tired brain struggled to bring the various events into one coordinate whole, the more jumbled it all seemed. And always he found himself back in Shanghai. Somewhere there the drama that was playing itself out in London had had more than one genesis. It was those of which he was still ignorant that held the answer he sought.

He was totally in the dark as to where Mother Hooly stood in the affair. He was guessing that she had had some close association with old Tom Ligan years ago; and there was some strange bond between her and Creed that gave that toughened veteran an air of composure and certainty in her presence. It was almost as if Creed had some call upon her which she could not deny. But that did not explain why Creed had stood by him in Shanghai when the foreign city, as well as the native city, whispered that he had killed Tom Ligan. Nor did it tell him why Creed had chosen to attach himself to him as a mere servant, to follow him to London.

Was Creed playing some deep game of his own? Was he using him—Dimmock— as a tool? And where did Hilda Grey come in? Why should she have tried to get friendly with him in the Willow Pattern Tea-house? Why had she hitched up with Sam Kiley and Nita Ligan only to double-cross them? She had fled through this misty dawn and someone had flung a gat round the corner and shot her down. Why?

He was bewildered, but he was determined. He would sit down and wait no longer on events. It hadn't been worth it—to skulk down in the country, not knowing at what moment the lid might blow off. He must get Kiley before Kiley got him. It could only be Kiley who had tried to put the girl on the spot that morning. Would she tell the truth? Would she live even?

He knew that the knocking that had so startled him and Creed had been the summons of a constable who had heard the shots, had suspicions but not of a definite enough nature to cause him to investigate too closely.

Mother Hooly had handled him successfully. It wasn't the first time she had bluffed the arm of the law. And while she was engaged with the constable, a Chinese boy was on his way out to one of the steamers in the river to bring back a ship's doctor.

Mother Hooly could have summoned half a dozen between Limehouse Beach and London Pool who would do her bidding and keep a close mouth. And by the time it was full day, by the time certain stains outside the alley door might have attracted the keener attention of the police sergeant who strolled that way, there was nothing to be seen.

The cobbles were washed clean. Three shots had been fired. One still remained in the girl's shoulder, to fall into the doctor's hand. One was found lying in the crack between two cobbles. A third was dug out of the heavy wooden gate at the end, where it had plunged after passing through the girl's side.

Dimmock found the girl conscious and willing, but not eager, to talk. She looked wan, her eyes still a little frightened, but more attractive than he remembered her. When he had touched her listless hand he drew up a chair. He felt awkward, tongue-tied, but he had to know.

"You are wanting to ask questions," he heard her say faintly. "I will answer them if I can. I am not hurt dangerously. You see, as soon as he began to shoot and I felt the first bullet strike me, I dropped and lay still."

"He—who?"

"Sam Kiley."

"I knew it. Why are you mixed up in this? Why have you been travelling with that gang? Why did you telephone a warning to me?"

"Not so fast," she smiled slightly. "I made friends with Nita Ligan because I knew she would lead me to you eventually. And I had to find you. I tried to learn something from you in Shanghai, but you eluded me. Then you disappeared. You see, you have something that belongs to me."

Dimmock frowned in sharp concentration.

"I have something that belongs to you," he repeated slowly. "What is it?"

"The box you took, or received, from Tom Ligan."

If Peter Dimmock had been entertaining any idea that it was his person or manners that had attracted the girl to him in the Willow Pattern Tea-house, or had caused her to warn him against Kiley at risk of her own life, he had his disillusionment in her last statement. A slow flush spread over his face.

"I don't understand you.". He said stiffly.

"I know," she returned, equably. "I will explain. I am Tom Ligan's daughter."

He stared at her incredulously.

"It is true. You would not know. Not many people know. Ask Creed; he knows. Tom Ligan married my mother years before Nita Ligan ever came to Shanghai. My mother was the daughter of a pilot in the Shanghai River. She was a strongly religious woman, and when she discovered soon after marriage that Tom Ligan was engaged in certain business which she regarded as dishonest, she left him.

"I was taken to San Francisco, then to Santa Barbara, where I was put into a convent. My mother, died, but left money for my education. I was free to do as I wished a year ago. I wrote to my father, but he did not answer. I travelled to Shanghai determined to claim my position, but when I arrived I learned many things.

"Then he was killed. I did not believe you had committed that crime, but I knew, later, that you must have taken away things of great value which Nita thought to possess. The money doesn't interest me; but I want the box of jewels. That is why it was to my interest to see you escape Kiley until I could make contact with you."

"You say Creed knew this?"

"He knew that Tom Ligan married Hilda Grey. He knows now that I am her daughter."

"What game is he playing, then?"

"I don't know. Ask him."

"Where does Mother Hooly come in on this?"

The girl looked puzzled.

"I mean the woman who runs this place?"

"I don't know. I never saw her before."

"Then what brought you here this morning at dawn? You must have had some strong reason."

"It was you. They knew you had a hide-out somewhere in the East End. Charlie Sin was trying to find it. He telephoned in the night that he had done so. I fooled Nita and escaped. I knew the time had come to reach you. Kiley must have discovered very soon after what had happened. He knew where to come—guessed that I was trying to get to you. I saw him running out of the mist. I ran into the alley. I didn't know it would take me to a door until I saw it in the wall. Then Kiley began to shoot. You must be very careful, for we must have a settlement. And now I think I am a little tired."

Dimmock rose at once. He made no attempt to give her any assurance. She might be slinging him some tale, he told himself. Yet he felt a little ashamed of himself that he could not meet the grey eyes that looked up at him. He was turning to go when he heard her whisper:

"I know I can trust you, and I'll soon be able to help again."

He swung back and laid his hand on hers.

"Don't you worry," he growled. "I'll not double-cross you. But we haven't finished with Kiley yet—nor Nita Ligan."

Stumbling along through the gloom of the maze of passages he felt his arm suddenly clutched as in a vice. He could see two, white-rimmed eyes glaring at him fiercely. He realised it was the giantess who had probably overheard everything that had passed between him and the girl.

"Come with me."

He allowed her to half lead, half drag him along until, all at once, they were in a small, square hall lit by an electric bulb. A pair of heavy portieres hung over a doorway through which came subdued sounds of clinking glasses and nullified, human voices.

Mother Hooly stared into his eyes searchingly, until Dimmock squirmed. Then she bent her huge bulk until her head was close to his.

"You play your game," he heard in a snarling whisper. "I watch. Now, look, and you will see something."

With that, she drew aside the portieres, disclosing the room in which the clients of the Sailor, Come Home danced in the evenings. At this hour of the day only a few lunching customers were there.

But Dimmock found no lack of interest in one table on this occasion, for, seated there as nonchalantly as if he had never slung a gat in his life, was Sam Kiley. And with him was Nita Ligan.

. . . . .

Dimmock walked down the room stiffly; as if he were treading on eggs.

He was no gunman. Even as mate of a tramp on the China coast he had been no bucko. If he had developed a tense caution it was because the events of the past months had forced him to draw on every latent reserve.

His first glance had shown him Sam Kiley and Nita Ligan. He didn't try to understand why Mother Hooly had pushed him into the danger zone with cryptic words. He didn't even know if he could count on Creed. Creed had done a fade-away.

* * * * *

He felt an almost unconquerable desire to loosen his shoulders, to limber his joints. Yet a semi-paralysis had seized upon him. It was a tautening of the nerves such as he had never experienced before, not even when he had sat in the sitting-room of the house in Sussex watching the green-frosted bulb in the fender wink its warning.

At first and for some steps he was only aware of the presence of Kiley and the Shanghai Poppy. His gaze was glued to a spot on the table between them. It seemed to give him a focus of both.

There was no telling what Kiley might spring. Kiley was sophisticated in all the ways of gundom. He had proved only that morning that he would sling a gat even in London and almost under the nose of a constable.

That took nerve. And it took greater nerve to stroll into Mother Hooly's and pick a table.

Pick a table! That was just what he had done. Dimmock saw that it occupied a strategic position. It was far enough into the room to cut him off from view of any stray person who might push open the swing leaves and glance in. And it was set at a point where a cool gunman could dominate the whole room if he was fast on the trigger.

Dimmock forced his gaze away from the spot on the table. He shot a glance at Kiley, who was sitting with one shoulder towards him. Kiley seemed quite oblivious of his approach; but Dimmock was as conscious of the gun he knew lay in the hollow of Kiley's left arm as of the one that nestled in the pit of his own. And Kiley might carry a Derringer strapped to his wrist, upside down, under the silk handkerchief that was pushed up the sleeve of his jacket.

He took in, subconsciously, that Kiley was dressed foppishly, flashily—grey suit, tan shoes, his hair varnished and plastered close to his wide, flattish skull. There was a diamond winking in his tie and, while he talked to Nita Ligan, one hand gestured, displaying four rings set with the same sort of gems.

The Shanghai Poppy was all in white. The pair looked airy, out of place in this low-ceilinged room with the artificial lights on at noon and every inch plastered with curios.

Dimmock's gaze swept the other tables. His tread became even stiffer as he saw Charlie Sin, Costa and Silva seated at another table, placed between Kiley and the door. Then, alone, at still another table that stood near the opening that led to the saloon bar, he saw Lee Yeng. The gang was present. What would Kiley try to pull?

Dimmock noted only three other customers in this room. They looked like "squareheads " or "bohunks"—seafaring men who would slide out from under if trouble started. They knew what a brawl would do to their shore leave; they didn't know that Sam Kiley, the killer, sat opposite.

Dimmock kept straight on to Kiley's table. He was close beside it before Kiley took notice of his presence. Nita Ligan had given him one indifferent glance just a few moments before. They were acting well.

Dimmock laid the knuckles of two fists on the table and thrust his head in between them. He was eyeing Kiley, but he was conscious of every movement that the girl might make.

Kiley removed a cigarette from the corner of his mouth, using his left hand. Dimmock saw that his right kept close to the cuff of the sleeve into which the handkerchief had been tucked. He knew now that the bit of silk concealed the ugly butt of a Derringer.

But Kiley's voice was perfectly suave as his hot, brown, killer's eyes turned upwards towards Dimmock's rugged countenance.

"Oh, hallo, Dimmock!" he drawled. "We came along to have a talk with you. Nice of you not to keep us waiting. Sit down."

Before Dimmock could reply something small and hard dropped with a distinct thud on to the table, missing Dimmock's head by no more than an inch. It rebounded against a tumbler with a light tinkling sound, rolled against a crushed napkin and came to rest.

Kiley, the Shanghai Poppy and Dimmock all stared at it. They saw a spent bullet.

Sam Kiley didn't move a muscle. Nita Ligan threw her head back and gazed upwards, as if she thought the bullet might have come from somewhere among the confusion of masks and skulls which decorated the ceiling, just above them. Dimmock shot out a hand, grasped the bit of lead, whipped round behind Kiley and dropped into a chair on Kiley's left, his back to the wall. Nita was now in the same relation of position to him that he was to Kiley.

The interruption of that spent bullet dropping from nowhere had acted like a switch on the current of tension that had held Dimmock in its grip. In one flash he seemed to get a true perspective of the inter-relations of the various actors in the drama that was playing to its final curtain in London.

He held the bullet between finger and thumb, visible to the other two. It was blotched with small, dark stains, left by its passage through living tissues or deliberately marked. Dimmock didn't know. But now he knew he must take a strong lead. He must bring Kiley to the point, and turn the trick before he himself was destroyed as the killer had tried to destroy Hilda Grey.

"Your property, Kiley," he found himself saying, with a cold, measured voice that surprised even himself in its complete control.

Kiley's right hand was still hovering near the handkerchief that was stuffed into his left sleeve. Nita Ligan had dropped a hand into her lap. Out of the corner of his eyes Dimmock saw movements farther along that told him Charlie Sin, Costa and Silva were watchfully waiting.

"What of it?" drawled Kiley.

"See those stains?" went on Dimmock slowly.

"Might be blood or—jam."

"You played a strong hand this morning, Kiley. You put a girl on the spot. But she talked before she—died."

Dimmock felt rather than saw Nita Ligan stiffen suddenly, then relax. Her eyes had left him, had passed from the bullet and were fixed on Kiley. Dimmock was giving every bit of attention to the killer.

Kiley ground the end of his cigarette in a saucer.

Before the other could get at his gun, Dimmock flung up his right hand and smashed the barrel of his own weapon between the killer's eyes.

"Let's get down to cases, Dimmock. Maybe I know something about that bit of lead and maybe I don't. It doesn't make any difference. You're not going to talk to the gumshoes. You can't afford it. So don't try to pull any bumkum on me. I came here this morning to have a showdown. I knew I'd find you all right. You'll find it worth your while to accept my offer."

"What is it?"

"I don't know how much money you got away with the night you bumped off Ligan. If his sorrowing widow is to be believed, then it

34

runs to a pretty good sum."

"You and she know better than I who bumped him off."

"Sez you! What was the talk in Shanghai?"

"It was a plant on me. If there was definite suspicion against me, why didn't they arrest me?"

"They knew all right. Political motives, Dimmock. The foreign colony didn't want a murder case in the Shanghai courts at the time; too much tension between the foreign element and the native city."

"Pretty smooth, Kiley. Go on."

"Well, I'm acting for Mrs. Ligan. She's here to endorse what I say. This is the offer. You keep the money, even if it was as much as half a million dollars Mex. But she wants that casket of jewels that you got away with. They are her property. Ligan had promised them to her."

"Is that all?"

"That's enough to go on with."

"I don't need to bother answering." Kiley's eyes came up slowly until they met Dimmock's. There was no other movement that was visible, but Dimmock could feel a something that told him Kiley was getting to the point where he would pull what he had come to pull.

"You get one more chance, Dimmock," he said lightly.

"And if I refuse?"

"You're going for a ride."

"You'll never make me talk."

"We don't need to. If we don't get that casket with what is in it, you'll never cash in on the stuff, Dimmock. I'm not going to waste much more time in London. But I'm not leaving until I've given you a ride you'll remember for some time after you meet the folks on the other side."

"Did it ever occur to you, Kiley, that I might get you before you get pie?"

Kiley flashed a glance towards the table where Charlie Sin, Costa and Silva sat. Then his gaze came back to Dimmock. The dark pupils were hot.

"I'm all set, Dimmock," he whispered. "All set for that ride. Do you come across or—"

Dimmock didn't wait for the finish of the sentence. He sprang for Kiley, concentrating on, his right arm. His left hand found the killer's wrist while his fingers were still clawing at the silk handkerchief.

His own right hand was dragging the automatic out from the pit of his left arm. He flung it round and pushed the muzzle against Kiley's side.

"Got you, Kiley, got you!" he panted. "Keep your gang off, or I'll blow you to pulp!"

Then the lights went out.

Before the other could get at his gun, Dimmock flung up his right hand and smashed the barrel of his own weapon between the killer's eyes.

WITHOUT the glare of the electric bulbs the place was plunged into the heavy dusk of an ill-lit cellar.

The mist of early morning had given place to a sun that was brilliant, for London. But little of that filtered through the obstructed front windows and scarcely an atom through the swing doors.

At first, it seemed even gloomier than widened pupils would have found it. But, to Dimmock, it was a sudden plunging into a cave of crazy gnomes.

He could not see Nita Ligan at all. Charlie Sin, Costa and Silva were beyond, towards the door. But he glimpsed ghostly figures running across the open dancing space, Lee Yeng might have been one of them; the seafaring men might have started to get out from under.

His whole attention was concentrated on Kiley. He had done what Kiley didn't believe he could or would do. He had got the drop on one of the fastest gunmen in the game. Kiley had underestimated him.

Yet he was puzzled and apprehensive. Nita Ligan could stab him in the back. Charlie Sin and the two Portuguese half-castes, had a free approach from the rear. And Kiley was still sitting quiescent. It seemed an age; but it was within ten seconds of the passing of the lights when Dimmock rasped:

"They can't get me before I pull this trigger, Kiley."

Kiley didn't answer. He wasn't even looking at Dimmock. He was gazing past him at something Dimmock couldn't see, but which gave vague outlines to Kiley.

Then, all of a sudden, a whistling sound came through Kiley's teeth. Reckless of what Dimmock might do he came to his feet, sending the table over with a terrific crash as he did so.

Dimmock fulfilled his threat. He dragged back on the trigger of his automatic. But there was no explosion. Only a dead click sounded.

He pulled again and again. Each time only that mocking tap of metal on metal answered him. Someone had emptied the weapon.

He heard Kiley laugh suddenly. He felt Kiley's wrist go tautly corded. He tightened his grasp as Kiley's fingers tore at his arm.

Then Kiley desisted. Dimmock could see better now, could make out the up-thrust of Kiley's elbow as he went for the pistol under his arm.

Dimmock flung up his right hand and smashed the barrel of his weapon between Kiley's eyes. The killer slid to the floor, and Dimmock flung round to meet Nita Ligan's expected attack. To his amazement she was nowhere to be seen.

But Charlie Sin and the two Portuguese half-castes were almost upon him. Lee Yeng was coming from the other direction. Dimmock jumped over the wreckage of the table and met Costa with a crashing blow to the face.

His arm came round, the barrel of his weapon catching the knife blade which Lee Yeng would have plunged into him. Charlie Sin was spitting out orders in coast Chinese that caused Silva to dive for Dimmock's legs.

The unexpected movement caught Dimmock unawares. His knees sagged as he struggled to kick Silva away. Charlie Sin jumped in with upraised arm. Dimmock couldn't see what he held, but he knew the next moment that it was as hard as his own pistol. The blow landed just above the ear. He went down into a world of spinning globes that seemed to crash together in one terrific, cosmic explosion that hurled him into depths of abysmal night.

A consciousness of a grey that was like that of primeval dawn crept into the black void in which Dimmock had been floating. His lids opened, but his brain was still too stunned to register visual objects.

He was almost as mindless and helpless as a sea anemone while fiery liquid coursed down his throat. Yet, each moment, the grey dawn was spreading, until it seemed to lift him into a world where he sensed the physical contact of things.

He began to grasp that he was an entity and as such could suffer physical pain. He began to realise that he possessed a head and that it was filled with hammering blows of excruciating stabs. His numbed limbs moved. His eyes began to send their telegraphic messages along to the brain that was asserting its functions more and more each moment.

Then came full comprehension and recollection He found himself lying on a couch that was hard to his shoulders. There is little wonder that the dim world in which he had been struggling had seemed peopled with creatures of frightful form.

Above him and about him were fantastic masks and grinning skulls, bloated reptiles and idols exaggerated into gargoyles. And, looming in the midst of them, one vast countenance that stared at him with eyes that showed the white of the eyeballs, in a complete circle.

There was something vaguely familiar about that face, or was it a mask? It was connected in some way with the world in which he had functioned before plunging into that amazing abyss of utter night.

Suddenly he knew it was Mother Hooly, spread out in a big chair, and that this was her private room. He became aware now that seated beside him was another being. He twisted his head a little and recognised Bill Creed. Creed had been pouring brandy down his throat.

He found himself trying to speak. He knew that his lips were moving, and his vocal chords struggling to express his will. But it was only a feeble croak that demanded of Creed:

"Who emptied my gun?"

Creed's voice was pitched low, but it sounded thunderous in Dimmock's ear.

"That's all right, Dimmock. I took the cartridges out. I had a reason."

"Hound," mumbled Dimmock. "Hound —dirty trick to play."

"You think so now, but you won't when you know the reason."

"Where's Kiley?"

Dimmock was struggling to a sitting posture and would not be denied. His mind was clear enough now, although his head still ached fiercely. But the full recollection of what had happened in the other room was spurring him on to anger and action.

He would have pushed himself off the couch, only Mother Hooly stopped him with a harsh command.

"You wait one minute, my friend."

Twenty-five years in the East End of London, had not got rid of the "chi-chi" slur of the China coast.

"Creed, he took away the cartridges this morning because I told him to do so. Do you think we did not have enough shooting here? Do you think I want the police camping on the premises? I've had too much trouble as it is."

Dimmock stared at her.

"But you knew my gun was empty when you sent me in to Kiley," he protested slowly. "You knew I was facing that gang with a dead weapon. Where do you get with that?"

"I sent you in there for a certain purpose. You hark to me. When you came to England some months ago I listened to what Creed said; never mind why, I fixed you a room here, and it was ready for you when you needed it. No sooner do you get here than Kiley shows up and tries to put that girl on the spot.

"I've got my own reasons for what I did, and for sending you into that room with an unloaded gun. Do you think Kiley would risk a shooting in there at that hour? He got away with it at dawn, when the streets were empty, but he couldn't pull it at noon.

"He wanted to get you out of the place and take you for a ride. The worst he or the others would have done was to knife you. They don't want to kill you—yet; not until they are dead certain they can't make you squeal. You did just what I planned you should do. If you had failed to face Kiley and tackle him you wouldn't be in here now. I'd have let Charlie Sin smash your skull to a pulp. But you stood up under the test. That's why you are here now. If Mother Hooly sits into a game she is going to know something about the stakes."

"Well, what about Kiley?"

"Kiley got away. Charlie Sin and Silva went with him. You settled Costa; Creed finished Lee Yeng; and I—I yanked Nita Ligan away from that table and through a panel into the wall just before Kiley kicked it over."

"You mean you—we've got those three as hostages?"

"You've guessed it."

"Who dropped that bullet on the table?"

"I did—from a little spy-hole in the ceiling. There are lots of those in this place. Nita Ligan guessed the truth."

"And you've got her—safe?"

"Safer than she's been for a long time," rumbled the giantess.

Dimmock rested his elbows on his knees and cupped his chin in his hands. It was beginning to appear to him that Mother Hooly had very effectively insinuated herself into the most prominent part in the drama that had been started by Sam Kiley.

Even the latter might be said to have been relegated to a subordinate place, for he as well as Dimmock had performed just as Mother Hooly had figured he would act.

To Dimmock, the affair began to appear more and more confused as each hour passed. He still couldn't understand why Mother Hooly should assume such authority. Why should she butt in? Why had Creed played her game and stripped his weapon of its cartridges? Had Creed double-crossed him? Were he and the giantess leagued together to diddle him out of the casket of jewels? Was his position now little better than that of prisoner? What would happen, he asked himself, if he should get up and announce that he was leaving the place?

He felt Creed's hand on his shoulder. The old-timer's voice had a note of pleading in it as he talked.

"I'm not double-crossing you, Dimmock. You keep on trusting me—me and Mother Hooly."

Dimmock flared into a rage.

"Trust you! Whose game is this, anyway? What do you know about the ins and outs of it? Do you think I am going to be treated like a child? Haven't I planned for months how I would meet Sam Kiley? What right had you to allow me to walk in on him with an empty gun? Who went through the mill in Shanghai? Who had to run the gauntlet of the whole foreign colony? Who had to stand up under the stigma of an accusation of murder? Do you think I'm going to play second fiddle now?

"I tell you I could have got Kiley out there as no one ever had a chance to get him before. I had my gun pushed into his side—one pull of the trigger and he was gone. And I drag back on a dead cartridge. I'm going to know a lot more than I do before I stand any more butting in by anybody. Get that straight. And I'll go after Kiley with a loaded gun this time."

"Well, if you feel that way, here's a little problem you can solve now," he heard Mother Hooly saying.

He looked up. He saw that she was holding out a bit of pasteboard which Creed took and handed to him. He turned a little so the light from the window revealed the name that was engraved on it.

"Major John Gisborne,
    "Shanghai Club."

Then, in pencil, he made out:

"Late Chief-inspector Sikh Police, Shanghai. Business—Strictly Private."

Dimmock looked at Creed, then towards Mother Hooly, who seemed almost to have disappeared into the voluminous folds of the stiff black silk dress she was wearing.

"What does this mean?"

"It means," said Creed, "it means that Major Gisborne is out in the saloon bar. He's been there for half an hour demanding to see Mother Hooly."

"But—Gisborne—here in London What does he want?"

"That's what we've got to find out mighty quick," announced the giantess.

A dark figure climbed softly from the boat and crept cautiously across the narrow jetty.

A CHINESE boy brought Major Gisborne to Mother Hooly's private room and closed the door after him.

The late chief-inspector of police—he was really on retirement leave and would not actually be posted off the service for another six months—was very tall and very thin until slightly stooping shoulders, gained, perhaps from constant dipping of his head to get through low native doorways.

His head was thatched with thin white hair, he wore a wispy white moustache, had a thin, high-bridged nose, thin lips and strong, jutting chin. His face was burned to the colour of mahogany; his hands were of the same colour; his movements quick, nervous—all marks of the man who had spent the better part of his life under trying suns.

He was faultlessly dressed in light grey, with a white silk shirt and neat tie. He wore low black shoes without spats, carried a light grey soft hat, yellow gloves and a very handsome malacca stick, all in one hand.

He had spent some forty years or more in the services, military and police— divided between South Africa, India, Egypt, Iraq and the China coast. He could speak sixteen Indian dialects and almost as many Chinese. He had behind him an extremely good record as a shrewd and capable administrator, and had piloted the Shanghai British colony with marked success through the stormy seas of the years of revolution in the country of the Middle Kingdom.

He had come up against a good many unexpected situations in his day, but, on this morning in the Sailor, Come Home, he received what might be termed a considerable shock when he recognised the person who awaited him in Mother Hooly's private room. There was no sign of the giantess or of Creed. They had made themselves scarce. Dimmock had insisted upon handling the unexpected twist that the arrival of Major Gisborne had given matters.

But, if he was surprised, the man of the police betrayed no sign. His voice was perfectly cool and suave when he spoke.

"You—Dimmock. I hardly expected to find you here."

"Nor I to meet you, Major Gisborne. Will you sit down? You asked to see Mother Hooly, but I believe I can satisfy any demands your business might take."

"You seem to take it for granted that it is connected with you, Dimmock."

"Not necessarily. Do you care to tell me why you have come here? You must be hunting something."

Gisborne took out a very handsome jade cigarette-case and selected a weed. He did not speak until he had lit it and sent a few puffs up towards a group of masks on the ceiling.

"You always were a little difficult to deal with, Dimmock," he said, at last. "For instance, I might have been of considerable aid to you in Shanghai if you had come to me. I knew you didn't kill Tom Ligan."

"Then why didn't you say so and clear me?"

"The moment hadn't arrived. I had suspicions, but I needed concrete proof. All I knew at the time was that you and Ligan were mixed up jointly in the opium smuggling game. I could have laid you by the heels at any time on that count, but it didn't suit my purpose. I was after bigger game. The murder of Ligan upset things more than you know. He was deeply involved with native elements, and I didn't want to stir muddy pools just then. Do you follow that?"

"I believe what you say. But—"

"Wait a minute, my dear fellow. I am going to place a few of my cards on the table—not all. I am too old a cat to be caught by a kitten. I know more than you think I know about the night you went up the river into native territory to keep an appointment with Ligan at his bungalow. And if you hadn't arrived about twenty minutes sooner than he expected you, you would never have got away with that wad of money and the casket of jewels. It is true, isn't it, that you did arrive a bit early?"

Dimmock stared at him wonderingly. It was perfectly true that he had reached Ligan's bungalow somewhat early on that fatal evening.

"That is so," he confessed audibly.

"It was a pretty slick plant that was arranged for you," went on Gisborne. "The Shanghai Poppy and Sam Kiley didn't overlook a single point except what Chance produced, and there were two. One was that you arrived earlier than expected, completed your business and got away; the other was—there was an actual eye-witness of the murder of Tom Ligan."

Peter Dimmock half rose from his chair. He sank back into it, trembling all of a sudden. If Gisborne were telling the truth —if he were not laying some trap for him?

"How do you know that?" he asked, hoarsely. "Are you kidding me, Gisborne?"

"I never kid unless I have a reason, Dimmock. On this occasion I am speaking straight. A Chinese attached to Ligan's household saw the old man shot down. The information didn't come into my possession until after you and Kiley had left Shanghai."

"Then it was Kiley."

"It was Kiley who pulled the trigger. It was Nita Ligan who led the old man to his doom."

"Why didn't this come out before?"

"Because the servant was afraid to speak. Ligan was mixed up in many ways with the native elements. In fact, to put it quite plainly, he supported a separate Chinese establishment. And when he first came to his senses after his crazy marriage to the Shanghai Poppy his first care was to transfer a large portion of his property to the native side so that she could not get her fingers into the pile. I'll tell you more presently, but I want to ask you a question and I want straight answers. Then I'll tell you why I came here to-day."

"Is it not a fact that Tom Ligan told you, when he gave you that casket of jewels, that he would have something more to tell you in connection with them on a later occasion?"

"Yes, he did."

"You see, Dimmock, I know what you brought away that night. The money is yours as rightfully as any money could be that was gained as you and Ligan gained that wad. We won't quibble about ethics now. But the jewels, Dimmock—they belong to someone else."

"Yes? Whom?"

"Tom Ligan's daughter—Hilda Grey Ligan."

"You seem pretty well informed, Gisborne. Who told you all this?"

"I'm telling you that this information only came into my possession after you and Kiley had left Shanghai. I know that this girl, Ligan's daughter, was in Shanghai for some time before he was killed. I know that she had approached him, but he refused any communication with her because he was afraid for her safety.

"He was inwardly very pleased that she had returned to seek him out, and as soon as he got clear of his entanglement with the Shanghai Poppy he intended having her with him. But he lived in fear every minute, as events proved he had reason.

"That was why he handed the casket to you, Dimmock. He was going to tell you later that they were to be given to his daughter. He never got a chance. But he trusted you, Dimmock, as he trusted no one else. I'm wondering why the girl mixed up with the Shanghai Poppy and went off with her and Kiley. If they discovered the truth about her, her life wouldn't be worth more than the snuff of a candle."

"Why did you come here this morning, Gisborne?"

"I am due to retire on pension in about six months' time. I asked for retirement leave for a definite reason. I wanted to follow Sam Kiley and the Shanghai Poppy to England and rope them in for the murder of Tom Ligan. I don't want that affair left unfinished when I come to the end of my term. It would worry me. So I have got myself temporarily attached to Scotland Yard.

"It is a curious thing that I was coming from the Yard this morning, wondering just what steps I should take to locate Kiley when I saw him with the Shanghai Poppy in a big car in Piccadilly. Fortunately I managed to trace them to this inn. It seems I arrived just after they had left. So I thought it would be interesting to have a talk with Mother Hooly. I have never met the lady, but I've heard about her on the China coast. It was she I was curious and anxious to interview now. I don't mind confessing that you were the very last person I expected to see when I was conducted to this room."

Dimmock nodded slowly. He was satisfied that Gisborne was not slipping him any bunk.

"I'll match the cards you've laid on the table, Gisborne. I can tell you quite a few things you don't know yet. Listen." He began with the warning that had been flashed to him the night before by the frosted green bulb concealed in the fender in the sitting-room of the house in Sussex. He related in detail just what had followed up to the moment when he had recovered consciousness in this room where they now sat.

Gisborne listened without interruption. It was only when Dimmock's voice tailed away that he spoke.

"You were a brave fellow to walk in on Kiley as you did."

"You can bet all you've got I wouldn't have done it if I'd known I was carrying an empty gun."

"Maybe not. So Kiley threw a gun on the Ligan girl; I didn't think even that rat would drop to that. I think I understand now why she hitched up with the Shanghai Poppy. There's character and courage there, Dimmock. Will she recover?"

"Yes. And you needn't worry—she'll get the casket of stuff. I thought she might be pitching me a tale."

"She's genuine all right. I don't think you need fear that Bill Creed has double-crossed you. Perhaps you don't know that, during the Boxer Rebellion in China, he was hauled out of death by Tom Ligan at risk of his own life. I fancy he would do anything to queer the pitch of the Shanghai Poppy if he believed she and Kiley were responsible for the murder of Ligan. I'm glad I found you, Dimmock, but— what are you going to do?"

"I'm going after Kiley and I'm going to get him. And there is to be no police interference."

"With such a valuable hostage as Nita Ligan there might be a chance to trap him."

"I'm not going to waste time on that. This thing has got to go to a finish between Kiley and me."

"Where does Mother Hooly stand in all this? Do you realise that there would be some very embarrassing questions if I told them at the Yard even a part of what you have told me? A girl has been shot and lies wounded somewhere in this inn. There is another girl, a Chinese and a Portuguese half-caste held as hostages. How would all that be explained?"

"You are not going to betray a confidence?"

"Perhaps not; but don't forget that I have come a long way to get Kiley. Besides, how do you know where to find him?"

"The Ligan girl will tell me."

"All right, Dimmock, I'll keep mum if you take me along. I must make sure of Sam Kiley."

"That's a wise decision," came a sudden interruption in Mother Hooly's throaty voice. "If you have any idea of taking your story back to the police there'll be another hostage held in this inn."

Both Dimmock and Gisborne swung round, to find the giantess just emerging from behind a curtain. And, at that very moment Sam Kiley and Charlie Sin were engaged in rounding off a desperate plan that was to ring up the curtain on the full burst of the drama.

Drawing aside the curtains, Dimmock saw his two arch enemies, Sam Kiley and the Shanghai Poppy, seated at a table. He knew that they were waiting for him. It was now or never.

NEVER, since he had achieved leadership of his first alley gang in 'Frisco, had Sam Kiley had things break against him as badly as here in London.

Kiley had reached eminence in his chosen profession by adopting an aloof attitude towards the actual commission of crimes. Not that he wasn't ready enough to sling a gat when occasion warranted; but he had taken a leaf out of the book of the big noises in Chicago and New York, had loitered in the shadows of safety while his henchmen turned the trick. It paid in more ways than one.

Nor, until he had landed in Shanghai, had he ever allowed any woman to intrude upon his life more than as the plaything of a moment. It had been his motto, again patterned after that of the big guns: "Never fall for a skirt!"

And, up to his visit to the Sailor, Come Home that day he would have grinned satirically had anyone told him that Nita Ligan meant any more to him than just what others had meant.

But the amazing truth had flashed into his brain when, with Dimmock's gun ramming the flesh of his side, he had seen Nita's shadowy form hauled from her chair by a massive hand and through what seemed, to him, to be solid wall.

It was this that had sent him to his feet, all unheeding of Dimmock's gun. Maybe he thought Dimmock wouldn't shoot; maybe he gave him credit for meaning his threat. He couldn't have said. He only knew that, for once in his life, he was willing to risk everything on behalf of another.

He knew nothing more after Dimmock smashed him between the eyes until he came to himself in the flat above the mews in Marylebone. He listened while Charlie Sin explained how he had made the getaway. He and Silva had carried him out of the place and slung him into the big car in which it had been intended to take Dimmock for a ride.

Charlie knew nothing of what had happened to the Shanghai Poppy. He thought she had reached the car until he and Silva got there and found it empty. They hadn't waited for anything, then. They had made a quick get-away, for they had seen Costa go down and Lee Yeng fall into Creed's hands.

Kiley knew it was no use to rant and rail. Charlie Sin had done what he considered best. But Kiley knew now that he was up against more than just Dimmock. He wished now that, instead of throwing the gun on Hilda Grey that morning, he had dragged her back to the waiting car with him.

That was a mistake. Still, Dimmock had said she was dead, so there was no use in vain regrets. The thing was—how could he rescue Nita Ligan?

The casket of jewels was no longer the major consideration. He was sorry now he had ever been bamboozled into this long chase to England after Dimmock. There were plenty of pickings in Shanghai, and this accursed fog-hole, London, was no place for a self-respecting gunman. The one time for months, ever since old Tom Ligan had been bumped off, in fact, that he had slung his own gun into play, he had opened up an unexpected game.

Who was this dame. Mother Hooly? It must have been she who had hauled Nita out of sight. And Creed—he had held Creed in contempt back in Shanghai. He thought he had hung on to Dimmock for some petty blackmail scheme and had lost his nerve when Dimmock cleared off the coast. But he had been very much in evidence that morning.

Kiley was uneasy, which was an unusual state of mind for him. And he was uncertain, which was an even rarer condition. He had had it planned to take Dimmock for a ride and make him talk. There were several little ways he knew that would make a man glad to start his tongue going.

Then, when he knew the location of the casket of jewels, he would have put him on the spot—whiff!—just like that. And there was a patch of ground under a heap of rubbish in the disused graveyard at the back of the mews which would make an ideal place to stick a dead man. No one would come across it for ages.

But that intent, except the actual killing of Dimmock, was all gone now. He must get hold of Nita and then make a getaway. Costa and Lee Yeng would have to look after themselves. But Nita—he'd have her out of that joint if he had to take the place to pieces.

He reached this point while pacing up and down the small sitting-room in the flat, smoking cigarettes as fast as he could puff them. Charlie Sin and Silva were in one of the other rooms, waiting. They knew better than to interrupt the killer when he was in this mood. But they came on the run fast enough when he called.

Just as dusk was blending into the darkness of a rain-soaked night, Silva sat huddled at the wheel of the big saloon car down in the garage.

Upstairs, Sam Kiley was just putting the finishing touches to his personal preparations for what lay ahead. Charlie Sin was gone, had slipped through the old graveyard early in the afternoon to prepare things in the East End for Kiley's arrival.

It was a telephone message from Charlie Sin, nevertheless, which decided Kiley on what personal equipment to choose for his purpose. It was the fact that, at the back or water side of the Sailor, Come Home, there were galleries somewhat after the fashion of the tiered verandas to be found in the native quarter and some parts of the foreign sections of Shanghai, that Kiley found what he needed in one of his bags. It. wouldn't be the first time he had approached a building in such fashion.

His flashy suit was discarded; his diamond tie-pin and rings had been put out of sight. Instead, he wore an easy-fitting suit of plain black, specially made for the concealment of weapons and other gadgets. His shoes were of black leather, with black composition soles that looked like leather but were, in fact, as soft to move on as rubber. A soft, dark-grey shirt and collar to match and a dark cap with an oversize peak that could be pulled well down over the eyes completed the essentials.

Before going down to join the waiting Silva, he took up the articles which he had got from the bag. Selecting one of them he took off one shoe and pushed his foot into a thinly fashioned but strongly webbed harness arrangement on the inside of which, just where the instep curved upwards, was a strip of black metal fitted with three sharp prongs, pointing downwards. The upper part of the harness strapped tightly about the ankle and when the trouser leg was dropped was completely hidden.

He refitted the shoe carefully, taking care that the sharp prongs should slip through a slit at the edge of the sole, thus allowing them to extend downwards until, when he was standing, the points almost touched the ground.

He applied a second such arrangement to the other foot and stood up, working his feet and pressing them to the floor until he was satisfied with the result. And, as he now stood, he was equipped with a pair of climbers, almost invisible, by which he could go up any ordinary post or pole with as much ease as a telegraph linesman climbs in his more cumbersome steel climbers.

There was an extra pair of the gadgets lying on the floor which he picked up and thrust into a side pocket. They would do for Charlie Sin in case of need. Then he took a last look round the room, patted the holster in the pit of his left arm where a fully loaded automatic rested, gave another touch to his right-hand hip-pocket where still a second weapon was in readiness, and, finally, slid his fingers up under the left sleeve, to assure himself that the double-decker Derringer pistol that was strapped butt downwards there was easy in its case.

He moved to the door with swift, silent tread. Even beneath the peak of the cap one might have seen the expression in the burning brown eyes, a look that reminded one of smoke. To-night Sam Kiley was out to kill. No subordinate would handle this job. It was a case where his own hand would sling the gat.

He switched out the light and went softly down the stairs. He got into the back of the car and sank into one corner. Silva needed no orders. He already knew just what he had to do. The big doors opened silently. The black limousine slid out into the mews; the doors closed. The hunt was on.

. . . . .

By eight o'clock the rain had settled to a steady downpour. It had followed the flood tide, and the prospects were all for a sticky night.

The Thames was about as dirty a thoroughfare as one could find. Even the river-police, in their wide storm capes and efficient new motor-boats that are fitted with cabins, cursed the blinding curtain through which duty sent them up and down, up and down on a ceaseless patrol for what the river might produce.

Yet not even the patrol boat out of Wapping, the senior and nearest station to the East India Docks, caught sight of a small, canoe-like craft that, clinging close to the wharves, found its way through the storm into the comparative calm in the little backwater behind the Sailor, Come Home.

The two figures who moved to the slow motion of double-bladed paddles paid little heed to the drenching rain. Among all the millions in London they were among the very few who welcomed the shelter it gave their purpose.

A shadow among shadows, the light craft was driven along until it rode close against the side of the long, narrow jetty, the extent of which was governed entirely by the width of the inn at the rear.

From the edge to the supports of the lowest of the tier of three galleries was only a couple of paces; and, away back in the days of the press gangs, not even that slight distance had lain between high water and the inn wall, for, underneath the more modern piling, one could have found the outlines of the ancient water-gate through which many a strange procession of men and cargo had passed.

Only one of the blurred figures emerged from the craft to cross the jetty. He moved with a certainty that revealed either a sound knowledge of what lay ahead or a close heed to minute instructions.

He did not choose at once to raise himself to the level of the first gallery, but, standing close to one of the supporting posts, peered through the driving scud at the warm glow that could be seen against drawn blinds. No sound of voices reached him where he stood, but it was obvious that the inn was warming up to the full swing of the evening rush.

From the water he had already noted that, on the upper floors, only one window showed a light. It was at the end of the third or topmost gallery. And this room but not the window was his immediate objective. Charlie Sin had given Kiley a pretty good idea of the layout of the place as he had learned it during the afternoon.

Nita Ligan might or might not be in that room with the light. It didn't matter so much to Kiley at the start. His aim was to reach that top floor and work his way down. If Nita wasn't in the room at the end of the gallery it wouldn't take him long to deal with whoever was there. For, he argued, Nita must be somewhere within those walls.

He began to mount, the sharp points of the climbers digging into the old wood with ease. His progress was as silent and as swift as that of a monkey going up a coconut tree.

He passed the first and second galleries without pause. On reaching the third he slid over the guard rail and took two soft-footed strides that landed him close to the window next that in which the light glowed. He did not bother trying to inspect that room; the blind was down.

Now he took from within his clothes some of the equipment he had brought along. Squatting, he laid on the floor of the gallery a square of coarse brown paper, a tube of sticky substance and a small diamond glass-cutter.

He brought the latter into play first. Under his expert fingers it took but a few moments to cut a semicircular line in the glass pane up against the sash just beneath the window catch.

Satisfied with the depth of this he dropped the cutter back into his pocket, picked up the tube, unscrewed the cap and pressed a good supply of the sticky substance on to the paper. Then he laid the paper, sticky side on, to the half moon of glass he had outlined.

A light tap did the trick. The section of glass came away clean, prevented from falling inside by the hold he had of the brown paper. He withdrew it carefully and laid it on the floor, pushing it well along so it was out of the way of a quick step coming out of, or going in through, the window.

He pitched the half-used tube over the rail and listened for a moment until he heard it "plop" into the water. Then he laid his ear against the opening in the pane and listened.

He stood perfectly motionless as he caught the sound of slow, heavy breathing. Someone was certainly inside the dark room and, apparently, sound asleep.

Kiley found a small pocket torch and thrust it through the hole, gluing his face close to the pane so as to overcome the glare that would be thrown back when he pressed the switch.

He took less than ten seconds to survey what the light showed him of the interior. He had seen enough, and now, instead of backing to the rail and retreating, he dropped the torch back into his pocket and thrust his free hand through the hole, searching for the window catch.

He found it, pressed it back and tugged gently at the lower sash. It came up without much difficulty. He eased it higher and higher until there was space wide enough to allow him to squeeze his wiry little body between it and the sill.

He made not a sound as his feet touched the carpet inside. He did not bring the torch into play again. He felt his way along cautiously until his outstretched hand encountered the end of an iron bed. He continued until his fingers found the shoulder of someone who lay outstretched on the mattress.

He needed no light to tell him the identity of this person. He had seen through the window. He knew that, on this bed, lay Costa bound and gagged; and that, on another against the opposite was Lee Yeng, in similar state. The gags accounted for the heavy breathing he had heard. He had stumbled on luck at the very first test of that elusive lady.

It took him but a few moments to release Costa and to whisper a curt warning in his ear. He parted with one of his precious automatics, the one he had been carrying in his hip-pocket. He would have to depend now on the other and the double-decker Derringer.

Costa waited while Kiley turned to the other bed and released Lee Yeng. The Chinese needed no warning. He knew what to do by instinct and long experience in the underworld of the China coast.

But Kiley did not give him a pistol. From under his waistcoat he took a knife, which was his last line of retreat, so to say, and pushed it into the other's hand. Lee Yeng was better with a knife than a gun, anyway.

Then Kiley led the way to the door, followed by the other two. What he found when he turned the handle was unexpected. He thought the door would be locked, but evidently bonds and gags had been considered sufficient, for it came inwards without resistance.

Kiley turned to Costa and Lee Yeng. His gesture told them to stand by where they were. He himself stepped out into a dark hall and turned his head to the right.

Under a door a little way along he saw a long, narrow chink of light. There came the faint sound of a man's cough. He made a second warning gesture to the pair inside the door.

Then he crept along towards, his objective.

In the mirror Dimmock saw the door move slightly—gradually open.   Then a hand
came through, groping stealthily.

DIMMOCK was standing in front of the old oak tallboy that was placed in one corner of the room.

At the foot of a small shaving mirror lay a few personal toilet articles. Among them, thrusting them aside with blunt, blued insolence, was an automatic pistol of heavy calibre.

There was no doubt now about whether it was loaded or not. Dimmock had attended to that with extreme care. Just as he had taken pains with the letter which now lay in the left-hand top drawer of the tallboy addressed to Hilda Grey or Ligan.

It was brief, but Dimmock had spent considerable time over it. It was only to be given to the girl in case he failed to return from his expedition to find Kiley and have a final settlement—one that would finish either him or the gangster.

Brief though it was it held the secret of the Ligan jewels. He had no wish, living or dead, to deprive her of those which, he agreed, were her rightful inheritance and to which her own efforts that had culminated with Kiley's attempt to put her on the spot had more than entitled her.

And now he was waiting for Creed or Mother Hooly to come up and tell him that he could have a word with her. Ever since his declaration to Major Gisborne that he intended going after Kiley he had been held up because Hilda Ligan had fallen into a sleep and on no account must be disturbed.

All during the afternoon he had fumed alone in his room, examining his gun again and again, re-reading the letter before sealing it up. Gisborne had remained below with Creed in Mother Hooly's private room. Yet the hours had dragged by, and still word did not come. Yet he was forced to wait, for Hilda Ligan was the only person who could tell him where Kiley's hang-out was located.

From where he stood he could see the reflection in the mirror of the door that gave on to the corridor. He was just about to turn away and drop into his chair once more when he thought he saw the door move inwards a little.

So slight was the impression that he could not be sure. Yet he retained his position and stood watching. A second later he knew he had not been mistaken. It was continuing to move inwards, slowly, stealthily.

His first thought was that either Creed or Gisborne had come up to tell him that, at last, the girl was awake. But then it flashed upon him that neither would enter in that fashion. There would be a preliminary knock, a brisker opening of the door. This action he was witnessing was that of one who wished to enter or peer into the room undetected.

Dimmock's fingers slid round the butt of the pistol and grasped it tight. He brought his arm away and lowered it, so that the barrel of the weapon lay against his thigh.

The door opened wider. A hand appeared, a right hand, as the watching man could see. Then the top of a sleek, black head began to take form round the edge of the door until a forehead came into view, a white forehead that looked strangely familiar to Dimmock.

He did not turn. He stood watching what was to follow as if fascinated. It was only when a face was suddenly thrust into view that the tension broke. For it was the face of Sam Kiley, the killer.

Dimmock flung round and threw up his pistol. It was done in the same fraction of a moment during which his eyes and Kiley's had met in a startled clash. Whatever Kiley had expected to find behind that door it was not Dimmock.

Dimmock's pistol crashed with an appalling shattering of the stillness. Kiley's face was no longer where it had been. A tiny plume of plaster dust showed where the bullet had plunged into the wall.

Dimmock leaped to get the bed between him and the door. As he stood now he was almost directly under the light bulb. The switch was close to the door, near Kiley's control.

And Kiley seized his chance. Despite the risk of a second bullet from Dimmock's weapon he thrust in his hand and pressed down on the switch. Dimmock took a snap shot at the mark, but darkness blotted out the result.

He moved to the head of the bed and dragged pillows and bolster in front of him. Poor enough barricade, but there was no telling what Kiley would do.

Silence, heavy, intense, portentous with weighty threat. He did not know whether Kiley had slipped into the room or was still lurking in the hall outside, waiting for him to make a break.

While he bent over the bed, tense, he was wondering if the sound of his shot had been heard on the lower floor. Would it bring Creed and Gisborne? Would Mother Hooly come cat-footing along to spring something unexpected?

His position was one of extreme disadvantage. He was bottled up in the room with no retreat. How Kiley had got in he didn't know. But the gangster had both advantage of stance and line of retreat.

Still that nerve-racking silence held. Was Kiley waiting to see whether anyone came from below? Or had he slipped away on some more important errand?

The Shanghai Poppy!

Suddenly Dimmock knew the truth. He knew that it was Nita Ligan who had drawn Kiley to the inn. It wasn't to put him on the spot that the gangster had invaded the place a second time.

Dimmock shifted his position a trifle. The slight sound of the movement settled the question of Kiley's whereabouts. Close to the door a shower of spitting flame showed as a sharp rattle of explosions broke from the gangster's gun.

Dimmock felt the bullets thudding into the bedding, ripping past his ears. It was a miracle that none found his body.

He began shooting as fast as he could work the trigger, using as a target the spot where the flashes had shown, though he knew Kiley must have been using the door as a shield.

He stopped after the fifth shot. He didn't want to leave himself with an empty weapon, and there was no time now to push a fresh clip in.

Still Kiley held his silence. Dimmock did not know that, for a few moments, he was free of danger. Kiley had withdrawn into the hall. He had motioned Costa and Lee Yeng to him. His hand was giving comprehensive illustration to his jerky orders.

"Down the hall—open every door—find the Poppy!"

Dimmock was forced to fresh action. He lay flat on the floor and rolled under the bed. If he could reach the other side he would be just so much nearer the door. On the other hand, if Kiley opened up, slinging his gun low, he could fill him full of holes.

Nothing came. He emerged on the other side and got to his feet. He flattened himself against the wall and waited. Kiley did not keep him long in suspense. The gangster was uncaring now if the racket carried to the lower floors.

He slid his hand round the edge of the door and opened up. The bullets zipped past Dimmock harmlessly. Kiley seemed to get a sudden idea that Dimmock had changed position. Two shots thudded into the wall less than a foot from where Dimmock stood. Pure guesswork, but uncomfortably close.

Dimmock had been counting the explosions. He figured that Kiley's gun should be empty. He might carry another, which would dispose of the advantage the empty condition of the first might give. But it was worth trying.

Dimmock came away from the wall, shooting at close quarters. The door slammed, the sound blanketing the click of the trigger in an empty weapon.

Dimmock released the useless clip and feverishly inserted a fresh-loaded one. He dragged the slide back to throw a cartridge into the breech, and took a step towards the door. He would go through the door and shoot it out, face to face, with Kiley. The thing must stop quickly, one way or another.

He found the handle and turned. No one tried to hold the door on the other side. He shielded himself with it as he drew it inwards, but no shot came.

He peered into the hall, a well of darkness. Somewhere in the near distance were sounds that told Dimmock doors were being opened and closed. There seemed no attempt at concealment.

His thoughts jumped to Hilda Ligan. Was Kiley searching for her? Was he even more determined to kill her than to kill him? Then Dimmock remembered that he had told Kiley the girl had died.

The Shanghai Poppy!

Suddenly he knew that even his life was secondary to Kiley's determination to rescue her. He lurched into the hall, to be almost blinded by a flash that seemed to burst close to his eyes. Something of terrific heat creased along the side of his skull, half stunning him. His sight was gone.

He threw up his pistol and shot—blindly. Came fresh pandemonium along the hall. He heard someone spitting curses close to him, felt a hand come into contact with his shoulder and drop away. Some instinct sent him swaying to one side. Through the paralysis that had seized his eyes he saw, vaguely, another flash of light accompanied by an explosion that seemed appalling in the confines of the narrow, low-ceilinged passage.

He emitted a groan and dropped to the floor. He was aware of an ejaculation above him; then came the soft pad of feet as someone ran down the hall.

Dimmock scrambled to his feet. He thought his sight was returning now, but he could not be sure, so black was the surrounding space. He put a hand against the wall and staggered along. His face was wet. He knew it was blood, not sweat.

His hand encountered nothingness, had plunged into an open doorway. He felt a draught of cool air on his face, and knew that he had found the place through which Kiley had gained an entry.

A shot sounded some distance ahead. Then voices, loud and demanding. He recognised Creed's harsh tones; he caught the smoother timbre of Major Gisborne's controlled voice.

They were smothered abruptly by the vicious rattle of automatics. Someone screamed, the highly pitched, hysterical protest of a mortally wounded man.

Came a terrific thudding noise, as if feet were beating upon a closed door or bare floorboards. Into the darkness was born a light. It fell on a swirling haze of smoke in which several figures seemed to dance grotesquely.

Dimmock ran towards the spot. Before he was half-way the figures broke apart, went this way and that, vanished; all but one that lay prone on the floor.

The light vanished before he reached it. He slowed his pace and pushed out a tentative foot. It encountered a body. Kneeling down he searched with his hands until he found a face. The features were broad and flat, Mongolian. He guessed it was Lee Yeng. But he didn't know whose bullet had sent him to his ancestors.

More slamming in the distance. Dimmock got to his feet and yelled Gisborne's name, called upon Creed. A voice came echoing back to him. Another door banged; silence.

Dimmock felt along the wall until he came to an angle. He turned it and felt for the floor ahead. His foot encountered nothing. He overbalanced and went crashing down a short flight of stairs, one of the many connecting links in the old inn.

Shaken, he dragged himself to his feet. The hot, wet stuff that had been oozing from the wound in his temple was getting into his left eye. His handkerchief streaked it across his face, but he could not see the fearsome sight it made of him. He stuffed the bit of linen into his collar and tried to find a switch.

Slipping through the window into the room, Kiley moved quickly across to the beds on which lay his bound and gagged confederates.

Dimmock never saw the stairs. Staggering, groping blindly, his feet suddenly encountered nothing and he pitched headlong down the flight, to crash on the landing below.

He encountered only a closed door. An ominous silence seemed to lie over the place. Kiley, Gisborne and Creed seemed to have vanished utterly. Dimmock did not know if there were any others. Nor did he know that Gisborne and Creed were lying doggo on the floor below trying to pick up Kiley's trail.

While he stood hesitant beside the door it opened suddenly. A body collided with Dimmock. He threw out his arms and grabbed an enormous bulk. He knew it was Mother Hooly, but he did not know that the door gave on to a staircase of whose existence few knew.

It was his voice that gave the giantess pause. Her great arms were threatening to crush Dimmock to a pulp. She moved away from him, and he heard a slight click.

Immediately the corridor was thrown into brilliant light by three bulbs that had been lit simultaneously from a master-switch.

Mother Hooly started back at sight of the blood-streaked man who faced her. But a fresh outburst of racket on the floor below caused her to swing round and run with amazing agility up the short flight of steps and along that corridor, flinging some indistinguishable words at Dimmock as she went. Dimmock caught sight of what looked like a length of lead piping in her right hand just before she vanished.

He went after her, caught sight of her rounding a turn in the corridor some distance ahead, for here, too, lights had been lit by the master-switch.

Dimmock was brought to a halt by the sight of a short flight of stairs on his right. He didn't know why Mother Hooly hadn't gone that way. But it seemed to him that the racket was not far from the bottom of them.

He plunged down them, and swung round the newel post at the bottom. Here was more light, and, coming towards him, he saw the half-caste Portuguese, whom he recognised as Costa.

Costa was running at top speed. He did not spot. Dimmock until he was a dozen yards away. Then he skidded to a stop, flung up a gun and began to shoot.

Dimmock's weapon crashed as soon. He was shooting faster than Costa. He saw the half-caste drop to his knees, still shooting, then, after a futile struggle to get back on his feet, crash forward, his face to the floor.

At the same moment Creed swung into view round a corner. He was coming along in a grotesque hop on his wooden leg, ready to shoot at Dimmock until the latter called:

"Where's Kiley?"

Creed recognised him by the voice if not through his blood-streaked features.

"Kiley's gone up another way. You've got this hound."

Dimmock didn't wait to answer. He raced up the short flight of stairs, reaching the top corridor just in time to see someone vanish into a room some distance along.

He ran to the door, found it locked. Holding his pistol almost touching it he pulled the trigger. The heavy bullet smashed through the old wood, shattering the lock.

Dimmock hurled himself against the door and plunged into the room. The light was on. He saw Kiley, small though he was, with a body across his shoulders. Dimmock knew it was Nita Ligan. He saw, too, that her ankles were bound; her head and wrists were hidden by Kiley's wiry bulk.

Kiley must have worked fast, once he discovered the girl. The window giving on to the outside gallery had been smashed clean out by a chair that Kiley had thrown into one corner when it had served his purpose.

He was over the sill and out on to the gallery before Dimmock was half-way across the room. Dimmock plunged after him. He couldn't take a risk with the gun for fear of hitting the girl; although he was remembering how Kiley had opened up on Hilda Ligan.

He reached the sill and jumped out on the gallery in time to see Kiley flashing a torch to someone beneath. Then he heard him calling Charlie Sin's name.

Dimmock reached the gangster and caught his arm.

"Got you, Kiley," he rasped. "Put her down. You won't need Charlie Sin."

Kiley let loose a string of oaths. Dimmock let go his arm and caught hold of Nita Ligan with both hands. He hauled her off Kiley's shoulder and let her tumble to the floor.

Kiley had gone for his Derringer. He flung it up in front of Dimmock's face and pulled the trigger. Dimmock had leaped to one side, and, before Kiley could give him the second barrel, his own weapon crashed down on to the gangster's arm.

Kiley hurled the torch into his face and rushed forward, Dimmock tried to use the barrel of his automatic a second time, but the blow slid off Kiley's shoulder.

He had a vision of someone coming over the rail of the gallery; caught a fleeting vision of Mother Hooly bursting through the shattered window. Then he felt Kiley's steel-like arms about him.

He dropped his weapon. It was useless now. He could do more with his bare hands. His predominating thought in these first moments was amazement at Kiley's enormous strength. His next was the realisation that he and the gangster were pitted against each other to a finish and no interference would alter the result.

He braced hard and sought to counter the hold which Kiley had got about his neck. It was a sort of unorthodox half-nelson. It felt as if a steel clamp had gripped the spinal cord, so terrific was the pressure Kiley was exerting.

Dimmock was forced to yield under that implacable force. His head came down, and, breaking away suddenly, Kiley brought up his fist in a wicked uppercut that sent Dimmock's head back with such force he could feel the paralysing shock to the root of his spine.

He felt a wicked tattoo of blows over his heart, in his stomach, and then smashing against the raw wound in his temple. It was the violent agony of the latter that steadied him.

He fell into a clinch and held on until he got bearings and balance. Then, when Kiley would break free, he let him go, tearing in with a whirlwind of blows that caught the gangster by surprise.

It was Kiley now who covered up. It was Kiley who sought another clinch. Dimmock met him, got his arms about him, and then put forth every atom of strength to break him.

He felt Kiley flinching in agony; he heard the gangster let loose a whistling sound that seemed to exhale his last resistance. Then the gangster went limp and, when Dimmock would have forced him to the boards, came to life again in one last desperate flash.

The force of his efforts carried them both across the narrow gallery. Before Dimmock could bring the rush to a halt, he felt himself thrown back against the rotten wooden guard railing. It cracked ominously under the impact, broke apart with a tearing, splintering sound, presented a jagged opening through which Dimmock and Kiley, still locked together, pitched downwards through the drenching rain.

It seemed to Dimmock that they turned over and over before they struck. Yet only once did they make a complete revolution before Dimmock was conscious of a terrific impact against his left arm, then he was in the water, going down, down.

Kiley did not attempt to hold him as he struggled. He slid out of Dimmock's arms, and it was more a mechanical act than anything else that made Dimmock grasp him with one hand as he fought his way back to the surface.

He came up close beside the light craft in which Kiley and Charlie Sin had arrived. He hung on while he gulped in great draughts of air to ease his pumping heart.

Yet Kiley remained limp in his grasp. Dimmock was still clinging to the side of the boat when a light appeared on the long, narrow jetty. He heard Creed's voice calling his name.

He answered feebly, though there was urgent need in his voice, for he felt a sudden swimming of the senses that threatened to overwhelm him.

The light came winking towards him, and now he could hear the tap, tap, tap of Creed's wooden leg. He was still calling Dimmock's name, but the latter could not answer. He was finding it more and more difficult to withstand the cloud that threatened to engulf him. Yet one hand continued to clutch the gunwale of the boat; the other still gripped Kiley. Had he died he would have been found as he was.

He was scarcely conscious of the hands that got hold of him under the arms; only vaguely knew that he was being hauled out of the water. Then he felt raw spirit coursing down his throat, and his senses cleared.

"Must have struck his head on the edge of the jetty coming down," he heard Major Gisborne saying. "Smashed the skull— well, that's the end of Sam Kiley."

Dimmock sat up, mumbling a question. Gisborne and Creed carried him in through an open window to Mother Hooly's private room. He never saw Kiley again.

. . . . .

Even Mother Hooly's ingenuity found it impossible to hush up the upheaval that had taken place in the Sailor, Come Home that night. It was due to Major Gisborne's authority from Scotland Yard and his statement that the matter was blanketed.

With Kiley dead and Lee Yeng and Costa in similar state the circle was smashed beyond repair. It was Kiley who was the vital link, though Charlie Sin was a faithful and capable pupil who proved his readiness to take chances when, during the excitement of rescuing Dimmock, he took a header from the top gallery and swam out into the rain-beaten river. It could only be assumed that he and Silva, who was waiting in the car at an agreed spot not far from the entrance to the East India Docks, made good their escape, for they vanished utterly. There were plenty of places in the underworld of East London where Charlie Sin could find sanctuary.

No case was made against the Shanghai Poppy. With the passing of Kiley, Major Gisborne was not anxious to press matters against her. She could not now benefit through the estate of Tom Ligan, and her part in that murder was only to be shown by circumstantial evidence. The actual proof had been against Kiley.

As for Dimmock, he was in the throes of too high a temperature for some days to care one way or another. But when he was able to get about he found it distinctly pleasant to sit with the convalescent, Hilda Ligan.

Needless to say, he took measures to have the casket of jewels, which he had received from Tom Ligan, handed over to her, she in her turn giving them into the keeping of Mother Hooly.

Major Gisborne came down to the Sailor, Come Home to see them often during those days, and he was in no way surprised when Dimmock informed him, in somewhat embarrassed manner, that he and Hilda were to be married.

But what did surprise the ex-chief superintendent of police was Creed's explanation as to why he had decided to remain in residence at the Sailor, Come Home.

"We were married in Hong Kong more than twenty-five years ago," he said calmly, referring to Mother Hooly, "and I guess it's about time I thought of settling down."

Creed and Mother Hooly! It seemed incredible, but it was true. And Hilda suggested to Dimmock that the hidden streak of sentiment which she had discovered in the giantess might have had something to do with her being attracted to an inn with such a suggestive name.

Nita Ligan vanished into the mists of the east. Many months after, had one been passing the terrasse of the Hotel Continental in Saigon, French Indo-China, one might have seen the Shanghai Poppy seated at a marble-topped table, her eyes inviting a burly Dutch planter from down Java way.

And, as he lumbered towards her, a fatuous grin on his broad face, keen eyes might have distinguished an undersized, Europeanised Celestial drift away through the shadows, a smile on his knowing face.

Charlie Sin was still tailing along.

THE END.

The railing gave suddenly and, still locked in each other's arms, the two men hurtled down into the dark river.

www.ingramcontent.com/pod-product-compliance
Lightning Source LLC
Chambersburg PA
CBHW020337130626
46549CB00003B/1200